Written by Renee Charytan
@notetokids
@reneecharytan

Illustrated by Rick Van Hattum
Edited by Laryssa Wirstiuk

Printed in the United States of America

ISBN-13: 978-0-578-43556-5

First Printing, 2018

Dear Family,

I love you more than anything else in the world.
Even more than sleep and hot coffee.

Thank you for all of the laughs, hugs, and most importantly,
for giving me the best material to work with!

XOXO,
Mommy–Wife–Family CEO

P.S. Sorry that there's "never anything to eat in this house!"

One day, a bunch of bewildered
children found letters instead
of their mommies.

Dear Never-Tired Child,

I'm exhausted! You need to start going to bed on time, so that I can finish my mommy jobs like folding laundry, washing dishes, and packing school lunches. I need critical adult time, to stuff my face with chocolate, drink wine, and binge-watch Netflix in peace!
And the sneaking into my bed every night needs to end! I cannot rest with your feet constantly kicking me in the head. If you want me to be on my best behavior in the morning, I need SLEEP. Please reconsider my wake-up time! My friend Sarah's kid lets her mom wake up way later. It's so completely unfair!

—Sleep-Deprived Mom

Dearest Toddler,

I realize that being a toddler is extremely difficult and draining! I can't imagine the intense frustration of not getting everything you want at the exact moment you want it! Having tantrums and throwing yourself on the floor seems exhausting! I truly empathize. However, at times you may be...well, just a tad bit...unreasonable. Like that time you completely freaked out when I didn't allow you to brush your teeth with water...from the toilet filled with your pee. Or the time you had a monumental meltdown because I could not turn the sun blue for you, as you had requested. As your mother, I love you unconditionally. But may I suggest that you get yourself together before I lose my mind and possibly sell you?

Love,
Losing-Her-Grip Mom

Dear Starving Children,

Since we have "nothing to eat" at home, even though I stocked the house with food yesterday, I'm going to the grocery store. I may be out for a while, but I will do my best to hurry back because I know you're starving.

I'm so sorry the seven meals that I prepared for you earlier were not to your liking. I deeply regret my decision to make you oatmeal, after you explicitly requested oatmeal. I can't imagine what I was thinking! Let me make it up to you by fixing you another meal when I get back. Did I mention the store is in the North Pole? I hear they have perfect popsicles!

Love,
Short-Order-Cook-and-
Buyer-of-Terrible-Groceries Mom

Dear Picasso,

I'm your biggest fan! You have my love, support, and encouragement always! I don't want to stifle your creativity, but would you consider...if it's not too much of an imposition...sometimes using paper or, perhaps, one of the hundreds of coloring books that I bought you? Instead of the walls?

Love,
Martyr Mom

P.S. Also, can you please refrain from coloring on our friends' walls? Not everyone can appreciate your art. Especially at your friends Charlie's house. We want to get invited back there! Because they are really nice and have really good snacks and a new espresso machine.

Dear Clingy Kids,

I love that we spend all our time together. But I could use some ME time. It would be nice to occasionally take an uninterrupted shower, and peeing by myself for once would be luxurious. Of course, I would love to watch every move you make at the playground. Watching you do your playground tricks is priceless, but I can't simultaneously pay attention to one of you flipping on the trapeze while another is hopping like a bunny on the other side of the playground! My peripheral vision can only stretch so far! And to be honest, I'm feeling a little worn out. I haven't taken a vacation or a sick day in, well, never!

Love,
I-Need-a-Break Mom

Mommy

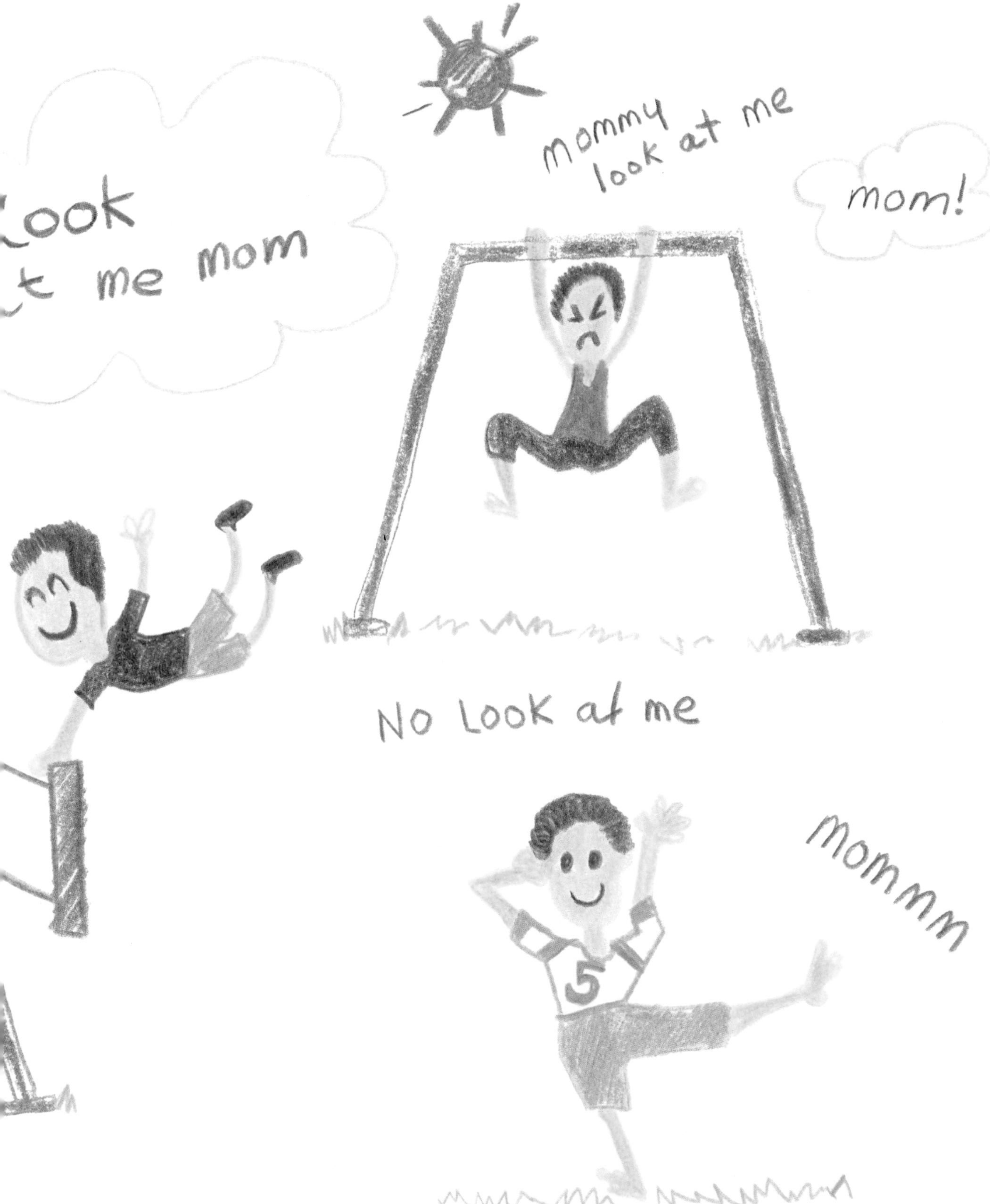
ook
me mom
mommy look at me
mom!
No Look at me
mommm

Dear Grandma's Angels,

Your mom told me your "wild" behavior has finally driven her over the edge, and she has gone to the spa to recuperate. She has left instructions with your sitter, Dad. Honestly, I don't know why your mom is always complaining! You are the most perfect, well-behaved geniuses that I've ever met! Anyway, please come visit soon and eat all of the candy that you like. You only live once, after all!

Love,
Doting Grandma
Kisses, Hugs XOXO

Dear Mommy's Devils,

I'm at the Sea Breeze Hotel. Not the spa! Grandma really doesn't listen. Anyway, change of plans. Dad has decided to meet me here and drop you off at Gramma's. You have exhausted your father (that didn't take long!), and he needs a break!

Love,
Haven't-Gone-Away-Since-
Before-You-Were-Born Mom

P.S. Be good at Grandma's!
Like the perfect angels that you always are for her!

P.P.S. Please do not eat too much candy!
Remember what happened the last time you went there?!

DEAR BABY,

YOU ARE SO SWEET AND CUDDLY AND HAVE THE FACE OF AN ANGEL. BUT I FEAR YOU MAY HAVE SOME ISSUES WITH ANGER AND VIOLENCE. YOU OFTEN CLENCH YOUR LITTLE FISTS, TURN RED FACED AND CRY INCESSANTLY. ALSO, SOMETIMES I FEEL LIKE YOU'RE USING ME FOR MY MILK. AM I MORE THAN JUST BREASTS TO YOU? PLEASE REFRAIN FROM BITING ME, SMACKING ME IN THE EYE, AND PULLING MY HAIR WHILE YOU NURSE. IF YOU CONTINUE TO ASSAULT ME DURING YOUR FEEDING, I WILL BE FORCED TO CUT YOU OFF YOUR SUPPLY. AND UNFORTUNATELY, THE MILK FACTORY WILL BE CLOSED INDEFINITELY.

LIVING TO SERVE YOU,
DAIRY FARMER MOM

Dear Four Year Old,

I love and appreciate all your handmade, heartfelt glittery school gifts. Nothing can ever compare to those. But could you also please consider getting me earplugs for Mother's Day? I love you with all my heart, but you're very noisy: your toys are noisy, your friends are noisy, and the theme songs to the shows you watch hurt my brain. While Little Bear is very sweet, I have an issue with Mother Bear. Do you know how much pressure it is to live up to her perfect parenting?

Love,
At-the-End-of-Her-Rope Mom

P.S Did I mention my brain hurts?

Dear Twins,

It warms my heart to see how close you are. I was concerned about your relationship for a while, like when you were punching each other in the face last week.

I just wanted to let you know that being a mom of twins is hard! I'm outnumbered here. And it's not fair that you two are always ganging up on me!

Stop teasing me! Or I'm telling Dad!

Love,
Outnumbered Mom

DEAR I'M-SO-BORED KIDS

I'M SORRY THAT YOU'RE ALWAYS SO BORED!
I WILL DO MY BEST TO BE A LITTLE LESS BORING.
HONESTLY, I FEEL TERRIBLE THAT THERE ISN'T
ANYTHING TO DO AROUND HERE! YOU HAVE
A PLAYROOM FULL OF BORING TOYS AND
NOT ENOUGH TV CHANNELS, OUR WIFI IS
PAINFULLY SLOW, AND THE IPAD IS AT LEAST
TWO YEARS OLD! I DO REALIZE THAT IT'S MY
RESPONSIBILITY TO PROVIDE YOU WITH
STIMULATION AND ENTERTAINMENT AT ALL
TIMES! IN FACT, I'M GOING TO TAKE THE NEXT
FLIGHT OUT TO SHANGHAI TO GET YOU THE
LATEST AND GREATEST THAT TECHNOLOGY
OFFERS! NO, IT'S NOT CHRISTMAS, CHANUKAH,
OR YOUR BIRTHDAY, BUT YOU DESERVE IT!
I'LL RETURN WITH BAGS OF GOODIES THAT
SHOULD KEEP YOU AMUSED FOR AT LEAST
A FEW MINUTES.

LOVE,
I'M-SORRY-YOU'RE-SO-BORED MOM

Dear Future Architect,

Your block structures are magnificent, and the Magnatiles universe you created is outstanding. And no, I don't mind you leaving your Lego city in the living room indefinitely. However, you may want to consider putting away the pieces that you're not using. I accidentally cut my toe on a loose piece. I'm sorry there may be some blood on that Lego. I'll try to be more careful next time. And I'm afraid my toe will need stitches. The hospital says I will have to stay here for a couple weeks to recuperate. I left frozen lasagnas in the freezer for you. So you and Dad should be covered while I'm away.

Love,
Don't-Miss-Me-
While-I'm-Gone Mom

Dear Sibling Rivals,

The fighting has to stop. I promise you there's enough oxygen in the room for both of you! You CANNOT steal someone's oxygen! And I don't care who started it! You are going to have to learn to settle your differences on your own because I've submitted my paperwork and have retired as referee, effective immediately. To celebrate this milestone, my assistant Dad will be taking me out for drinks tonight. Please do not wait up.

Former-Referee Mom

Well, the poor children just wanted their mommies back. Who would tuck them in at night, kiss their boo boos, wipe their butts? Who would hold all their garbage or buy terrible groceries?

They needed a plan. But how could they make one themselves? Mom made all the plans. They went to Dad, but he didn't know either. So, they texted Grandma, and she knew what to do...

…Grandma organized
an epic playdate where
the children played,
ran wildly, and made
massive messes,
while the mommies
laughed, cried,
and shared stories.

And then the mommies came home.
Why?

Because mommies always come home.
Because they love their children
more than anything else in the world.
Even more than sleep and hot coffee.

ACKNOWLEDGMENTS

To my husband, Ariel, thank you for being my biggest fan, toughest critic, and best friend (since eighth grade). And for marrying me even after seeing the inside of my locker!

To my sweet children, Ayla, Harry, and Eve. Thank you for making me a mother. I am your biggest fan. Sorry for all the yelling while I was editing this book!

To my Poodle, Petunia, thank you for all the snuggles, for never judging, for always listening, and never talking.

To my tortoise, Eloise, thank you for never complaining. You are a kick-ass turtle.

To Rick, thank you for continuing to partner with me and for all of your wonderful illustrations.

To my editor, Laryssa, thank you for reminding me that grammar is an "actual thing." And for always going above and beyond.

To my graphic designer and dear friend, Amber, you rock! Working with you has been an honor. Thanks for everything!

To my publicist, Louis, thank you for keeping me somewhat sane and for making work fun. We always have so much to talk about, and it's amazing we get anything done!

To my Pilates instructor/photographer/shenanigan accomplice and sweet friend, Jody, thank you for all of your ideas and suggestions. You are the best!

To all my readers, fans, and followers, you are my people. Thank you for your continued support and for inspiring me every single day!